Lei
Day

Photographed by
Minako Ishii

www.beyondbordersimages.com

Written by
Jeffrey Kent

3565 Harding Avenue
Honolulu, Hawai'i 96816
toll free: (800) 910-2377
phone: (808) 734-7159
fax: (808) 732-3627
e-mail: sales@besspress.com
www.besspress.com

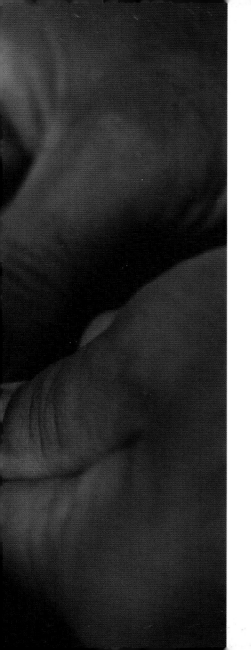

Lei Day is a celebration of the Hawaiian art of lei-making, and the spirit of giving and receiving a lei. This custom of lei-making is as old as the ancient Hawaiians that first discovered these islands.

A lei can be made from almost anything. The most common lei come from nature and is usually made out of flowers, leaves, nuts, and berries. Feathers and seashells are used as well.

On Lei Day, the lei are made to represent the lei of the eight major Hawaiian islands.

A red lei represents the island of Hawai'i's *'Ohi'a Lehua* flower.

A pink lei represents the island of Maui's *Lokelani* flower.

Of the eight major islands represented, this is the only plant that is not indigenous to Hawai'i.

A silvery-gray lei represents the island of Kaho'olawe's *Hinahina* plant. This beautiful little plant can be found amongst the rocks down by the shoreline.

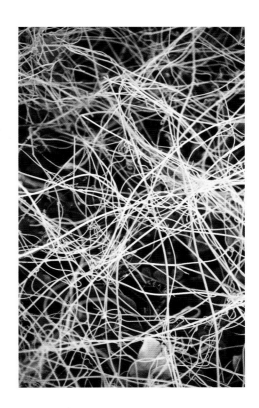

An orange lei represents the island of Lana'i's *Kauna'oa* vine. Twisted together, the *Kauna'oa* vines create a beautiful lei.

A silvery-green lei represents the island of Moloka'i's *Kukui* nut, leaf and flower.

Kukui nuts strung together create a lei popular with boys.

A yellow lei represents the island of O'ahu's *'Illima* flower.

It takes hundreds of *'Illima* flowers strung closely to creat a single strand of this lei.

A purple lei represents the island of Kaua'i's *Mokihana* berry.

This berry can only be found on the island of Kaua'i. Strung together, they create a special lei very special occasions.

And finally the white lei represents the island of Ni'ihau's *Pūpū* (shell).

A lei made of Ni'ihau's *Pūpū* (shells) was considered to be Queen Emma's favorite lei.

The Hawaiian art of lei-making has been passed down for centuries from the *kokua* (help) of older generations sharing their wisdom. This passing down of knowledge ensures the art of lei-making will grow and prosper.

Lei are waiting to be made, so take a good look around you. Imagine a leaf from a plant or a flower from a tree made into a lei that you can wear.

To begin, you will need to collect your lei material from your surrounding trees, flowers, and bushes. Please take only what you need and remember that Mother Nature wore flowers long before mankind.

There are many ways to make a lei, but the *kui* (stringing) method is the best to start off with. It's simple and can be done with just a lei needle tied to a string.

You will need to set your material on a table in front of you in the order that you plan to string them. Concentrate and be careful as you thread your needle through the center of your flower, leaf, nut, or berry, and pull them down your string. When your lei is complete, tie the end of the strings together.

Congratulations! You are finished. Now you may wear your lei.

And with their lei of aloha, they gently make a final offering to Hawai'i's royal past.

On the following day, the prize winning lei are brought to the Royal Burial Grounds. The Lei Queen and the Lei Princesses select their favorite lei.

Hawaiian musicians, hand crafters, and Hula Hālau also celebrate the newly crowned Lei Queen and her Lei Princesses.

Hula performers wear lei and dance hula in honor of the Lei Queen, Lei Princesses, and Lei Day.

Each year, the selection of the Lei Queen rotates between three different categories; *Nā Wahine Ōpio* (The Young Women), *Nā Mākuahine* (The Adult Women), and *Nā Kupunahine* (The Grandmothers).

On this day, both *keiki* and adult lei makers, participate in a competition to see who can make the most beautiful lei.

The most special Lei Day celebration is held in Honolulu at Queen Kapi'olani Park, where the spirit of aloha takes center stage. It is a day to remember Hawai'i's past while celebrating its future.

A May Day Queen and King are selected along with a royal court to represent the Hawaiian Kingdom of old. The eight major islands are represented by the royal court; Hawaiʻi (Red), Maui (Pink), Oʻahu (Yellow), Molokaʻi (Green), Kahoʻolawe (Gray), Kauaʻi (Purple), Niʻihau (White), and Lanaʻi (Orange).

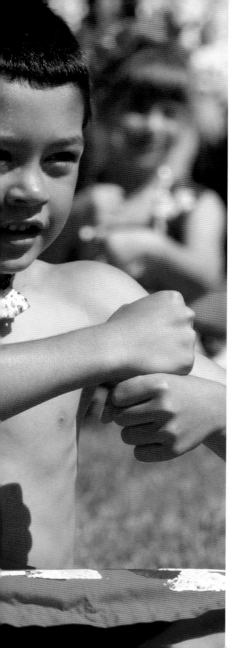

In celebration of Lei Day, school children throughout the islands learn about the many customs and cultures found in Hawai'i.

Today, Lei Day is a very special opportunity to honor the Hawaiian custom of expressing aloha by making, giving, and receiving lei.

In 1928, the first Lei Day celebration was held in Honolulu. The traditions of exchanging May baskets and May pole dances were blended into the Hawaiian customs of sharing lei and hula. And thus the phrase was coined "May Day is Lei Day in Hawai'i".

In Brentham England, May Day is celebrated with a procession of young maidens wearing flower garlands and carrying beautiful bouquets. They are joined by young boys dressed as English characters. Every year they crown a new May Day Queen.

In fact, Hawai'i's Lei Day comes from the traditional version of May Day that originated over 700 years ago in England, with the displaying of May flowers and May Pole Dances.

Photograph by Werner Stoy, Camera Hawaii, Courtesy Bishop Museum

This mutual respect was shown when Queen Kapi'olani and the future Queen Liliu'okulani visited England to celebrate Queen Victoria's Coronation Jubilee. It was shown again when England's Queen Mother danced with Hawai'i's Duke Kahanamoku.

Since the very beginning of King Kamehameha the Great's rule, the Kingdoms of Hawai'i and Great Britain have shared a mutual admiration for celebrations, royalty, and flowers.

This book is dedicated to Angel and the children at Maili land.

Acknowledgments

The theme of this book has been on my mind for quite awhile as I took many photographs of the Lei Day celebration organized by the City and County of Honolulu. It is such a beautiful tradition that has gone through a big transition from its English roots to the Hawaiian version enjoyed today. While I was shooting at Lei Day in 2007, some students from Waiau Elementary School randomly ran up to me and presented me with leis that they had made and said, "Aloha, my teacher said today is a day to share aloha!" It warmed up my heart and made me yearn for the traditions of old Hawai'i. It is the author's and my strong wish that this book will help inspire children to carry on the traditions of Lei Day, as they share their aloha with loved ones and strangers.

This book could not have been completed without the generous support of many people. Our sincere gratitude goes out to Kaiulani and Gina of the City and County of Honolulu, the lei queens and lei princesses who have made this day very special, to Diane, who runs keiki lei making workshops, to Sue and Pat from the Brentham Society who assisted us with great hospitality and shared their very traditional English May Day with us. Heartful thanks to all the lei makers, hula dancers, and musicians who helped add the colorful images to this book; the Choy brothers, Alama Hula Studio, Hālau Hula O Hōkūlani, Nā Wahine O Ka Hula Mai Ka Pu'uwai, Hula Hālau Nā 'Ōpio O Ko'olau, Hālau Lōkahi Public Charter School and the Makaha Sons. Special thanks to Sunset Elementary School and Punahou School for sharing their May Day celebration with us.

Design: Carol Colbath

Cataloging-in-publication data

Ishii, Minako.
  May Day/Lei Day / Minako
Ishii.
        p.   cm.
  Includes illustrations.
  ISBN: 978-1-57306-288-6
  1. May Day — Hawaii — Pictorial works —
Juvenile literature. 2. Leis — Hawaii —
Pictorial works — Juvenile literature.
3. Pageants — Hawaii — Pictorial works —
Juvenile literature. 4. Festivals - Hawaii —
Pictorial works — Juvenile literature.
5. Hawaii — Social life and customs ——
Pictorial works — Juvenile literature.
6. Flowers — Hawaii — Pictorial works —
Juvenile literature. I. Title.
GT4945.I84 2008 394.2627-dc22

Printed in China

May Day

Photographed by
Minako Ishii

www.beyondbordersimages.com

Written by
Jeffrey Kent

3565 Harding Avenue
Honolulu, Hawai'i 96816
toll free: (800) 910-2377
phone: (808) 734-7159
fax: (808) 732-3627
e-mail: sales@besspress.com
www.besspress.com